This book belongs t

Pinkalicious

SCHOOLTASTIC
STORYBOOK FAVORITES

by Victoria Kann

HARPER
An Imprint of HarperCollinsPublishers

Table of Contents

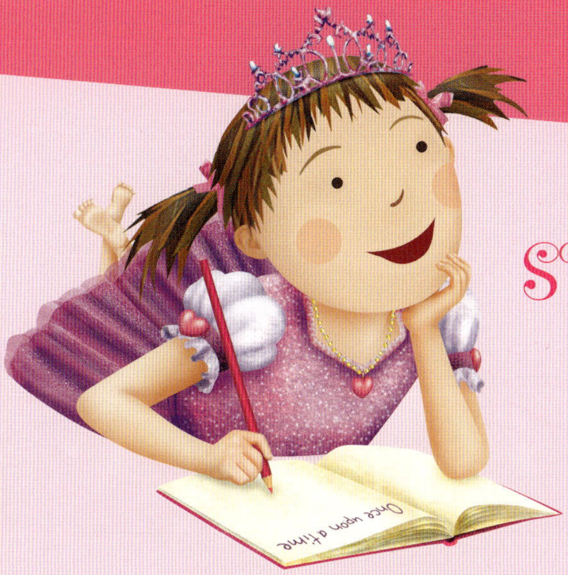
Once upon a time

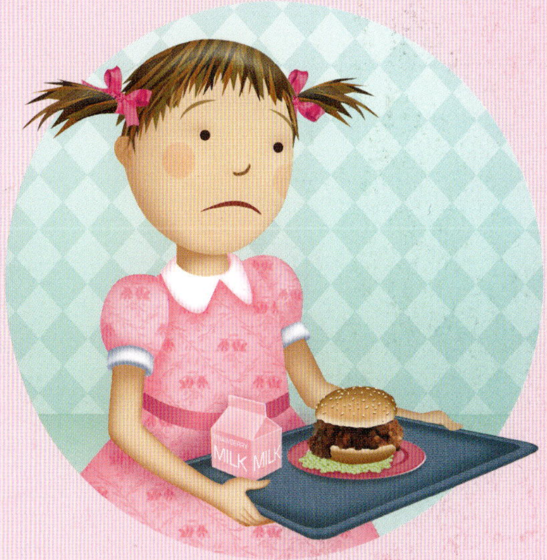

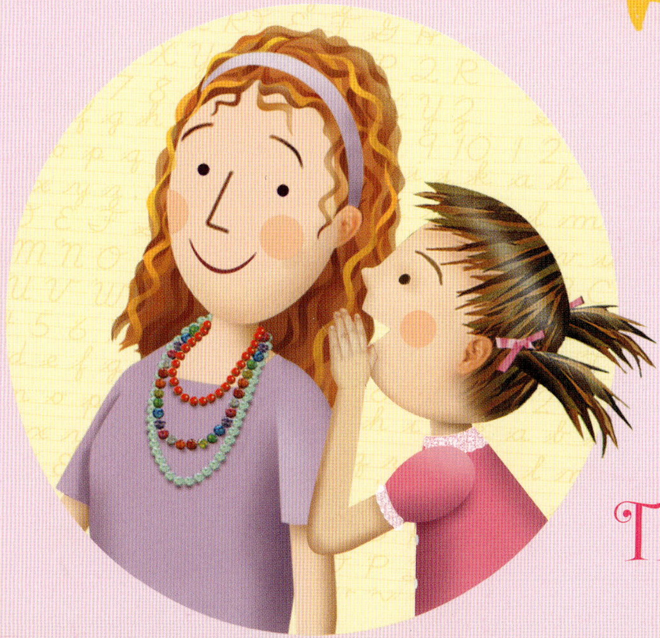

To Zelda, Grace, and David
—V.K.

Pinkalicious®

School Rules!

by Victoria Kann

School is okay.

Except for one thing.

When I am at school,

I miss Goldilicious.

Goldie, for short.

Goldie is my unicorn.

I really like my teacher.

His name is Mr. Pushkin.

I have some friends in my class

and I made a new friend yesterday.

But I miss Goldie anyway.

This morning when I woke up

I had a very good idea.

I could bring Goldie to school with me!

School would be
perfectly pinkatastic
with Goldilicious
there, too.

There was a shiny red apple

on Mr. Pushkin's desk.

Goldie took the apple
and nibbled it gently.

Mr. Pushkin heard Goldie munching
and he thought it was me.
"Pinkalicious, there is no eating
until snack time," he said.
"It's the rule."

"It's not me," I said.

"It's Goldilicious, my unicorn!

She didn't eat much for breakfast,"

I added.

Mr. Pushkin smiled.

He took me aside

and he told me that unicorns

are not allowed in school.

"It's the rule," he said.

Rules are something

I do not love about school.

And I really do not love

the rule about no unicorns.

I began to cry a little.

I cried a little harder.

"Okay, Pinkalicious,"
said Mr. Pushkin.
"Your unicorn may stay,
just this once."

I stopped crying.
In fact, I clapped
and twirled.

"But if your unicorn stays, you must teach her the rules," Mr. Pushkin said. "Do you think you can do that?"

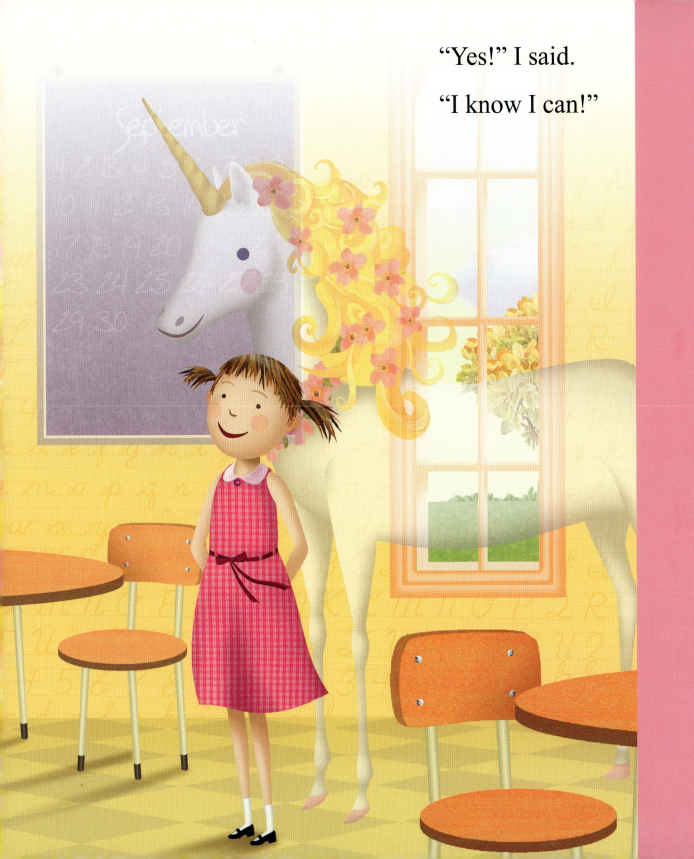

"Yes!" I said.

"I know I can!"

At reading time,

Goldilicious was very quiet.

Goldilicious helped me with my math.

Unicorns are very good at counting.

When it was time for recess,

I showed Goldilicious

how to line up by the door.

Goldilicious did not push

or wiggle or cut the line at all.

Goldilicious played nicely

with the other kids.

Everyone had so much fun
with Goldie and me.

I didn't know I had so many friends at school!

Soon it was time to go home.

Goldie got my backpack

off its hook.

"Tell me, Pinkalicious,"

said Mr. Pushkin.

"Did you and your unicorn

have a good day?"

"We sure did!" I said.

"School rules!"

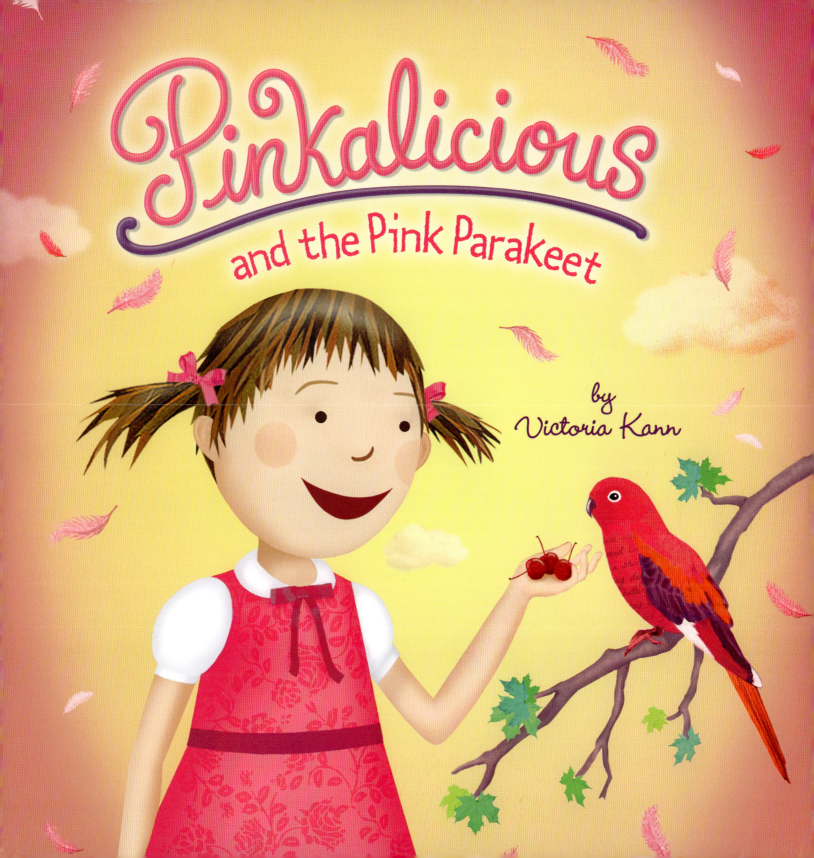

Pinkalicious

and the Pink Parakeet

by

Victoria Kann

To Brigitte, with love

and the Pink Parakeet

by Victoria Kann

It was Bird Week at school,

my favorite week ever!

Every day my class

learned fun facts about birds.

I told my family everything I learned.

"Fact," I told Mommy.

"Hummingbirds can fly backward."

"Fact," I told Daddy.

"Robin eggs are blue."

"Fact," I told Peter.

"Orioles can eat

seventeen worms in a minute."

"Big whoop," he said.

"So can I."

The last day of Bird Week was the best one yet.

My class went on a field trip

to the house of birds at the zoo!

On the bus, I took out my bird book.
I flipped through the pages
and saw something amazing.

"Fact," I cried.

"There's a pink parakeet!

It's small and sweet

and pinkerrifically pink!"

"Yes," said Ms. Penny,

"but it's a very rare bird.

You may not see one today."

I wasn't so sure about that.

I was really good at bird-watching.

When we got to the house of birds,

I couldn't believe my eyes.

I saw one red parrot,

two blue peacocks,

six green-and-yellow lovebirds,

and a toucan with an orange beak.

But not a single pink parakeet.

Soon it was time to leave.

"I'm sorry, Pinkalicious,"
Alison said.

"Maybe you'll see one another day."

We started walking out together,

but just as we got to the door,

I heard a strange call.

"Pink, pink, pink, PINK!"

"What was that?" I said.

"Pink, pink, pink, PINK!"

Alison and I looked at each other.

"The parrot!" we cried.

We ran over to the parrot's perch.

"He's telling us something," I said.

The parrot lifted its wing.

It was pointing to the door.

"Pink, pink, pink, PINK!" it called.

A pink parakeet!

At last, I saw one.

It was right inside

Ms. Penny's hood!

"Wait, Ms. Penny!"

I called.

But she was already

out the door.

HOUSE OF BIRDS

By the time we caught up to
Ms. Penny, it was too late.
Her hood was empty.
The bird was gone.

I was so upset.

I told Ms. Penny what happened.

"Maybe it didn't fly far," she said.

Together, the whole class searched

for the missing pink parakeet.

Everyone scanned the treetops,

but the leaves were too thick.

We looked through the bushes,

but we didn't see a thing.

I was about ready to give up

when I remembered my bird book.

I read about the parakeet again

and came up with a plan.

"'Fact,'" I read out loud.

"'Pink parakeets eat fruit.'

Who has a snack?"

Molly had cherries from lunch.

"'Fact,'" I said.

"'They also like taking baths.'"

Jack filled a small dish with water.

We put everything together.

"There's one last fact," I said.

"These parakeets tweet a lot.

So here goes . . . !"

I closed my eyes
and thought pink thoughts.
Then I whistled my very best
pinkerrific birdcall.

Suddenly, I heard wings flapping.

My classmates gasped.

I opened my eyes, and there it was!

The pink parakeet was eating fruit

while taking a bath.

Ms. Penny picked up
the parakeet gently
and brought it back to the birdhouse.
The whole class cheered!

When she came back, Ms. Penny laughed.

"Pinkalicious saved the day," she said.

"And that's a fact!"

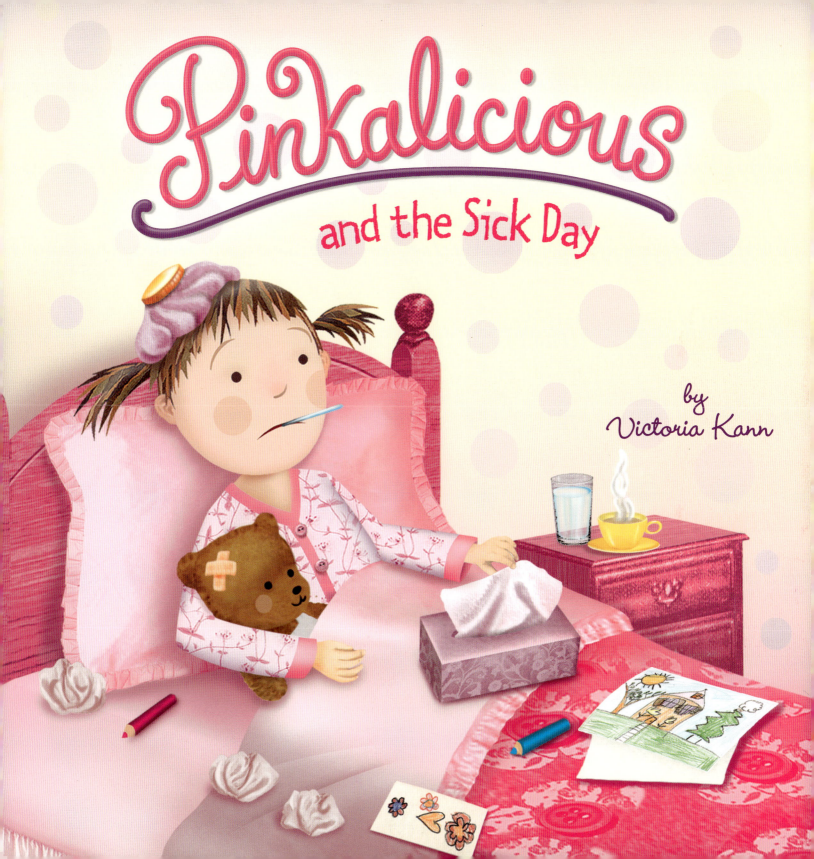

To all the school nurses
who take care of our children.
Thank you!
—V.K.

Pinkalicious

and the Sick Day

by Victoria Kann

When the bell rang

at the end of the day,

Principal Hart handed me a letter.

"Give this to your mom," she said.

Uh-oh. Was I in trouble?

When I got home,
I found Mommy.
I waited while she
read the letter.

Mommy smiled.

"You have perfect attendance.

Tomorrow you get to be

principal for the day," she said.

"I'm very proud of you!"

"Yippee!" I yelled.

"I'm in charge.

No homework!"

"I don't know about that,"
Mommy said.

"However, you do get to read
the morning announcements
and eat lunch with Principal Hart."

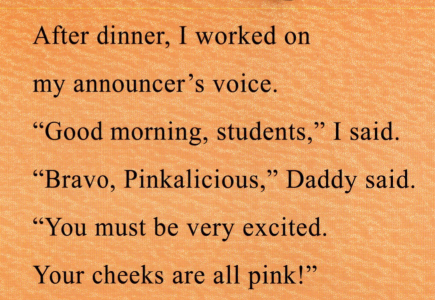

After dinner, I worked on

my announcer's voice.

"Good morning, students," I said.

"Bravo, Pinkalicious," Daddy said.

"You must be very excited.

Your cheeks are all pink!"

I nodded.

I was excited,

but I was also very sleepy.

I went to bed early.

When I woke up, my head hurt.

My eyes itched.

My throat felt scratchy.

ACHOO! ACHOO! ACHOO!

Daddy took my temperature.

"You have a fever," he said.

"No school for you today."

He tucked me back into bed.

Then I remembered.

"I HAVE to go to school," I said.

"I'm principal for the day!"

"I'm sorry, Pinkalicious,"

Mommy said.

"I will make you some tea,"
said Mommy.

Daddy tried to cheer me up.

He put my favorite books on my bed.

Then he gave me a big hug,

and I went back to sleep.

I woke up feeling a bit better,

but I still had the sniffles.

I looked in the mirror.

My nose was perfectly pink!

Mommy came in with pink tea.

"My mom used to make this

for me when I was sick," she said.

"It's elderberry tea."

I took a sip. Yum!

I got to stay in my pajamas all day!

Mommy brought me crayons,

and I colored in bed.

I drew a picture
of me riding Goldie to school.

Daddy called from work

to see how I was.

He told me a joke to make me laugh.

"Why did the pink panda

go to the doctor's office?

Because she was pink!"

I giggled, but I was still a little
sad because I wasn't at school.
I would not be able to share
the joke at recess.

In the afternoon, the phone rang.

It was Principal Hart!

"I'm home sick, too," she said.

"When you come back,

you can still

be principal for the day."

I felt a pinka-million times better.

Then Peter came home.

"Guess what I did today?" I said.

"I colored and I read books.

Mommy made me pink tea,

and I didn't even

have to get dressed!"

"I want to be sick, too!" said Peter.

Then he smelled my cold medicine.

"Yuck, forget it!" he said.

I giggled.

The next morning,
my nose was a normal color
and I felt all better.
"Your temperature is normal,"
Mommy said. "You can go to
school today."
"Yay!" I cheered.

When I got to school,

I went straight to the office.

I couldn't wait to tell everyone

the joke about the pink panda!

"Good morning," I said.

"This is Principal Pinkalicious!"

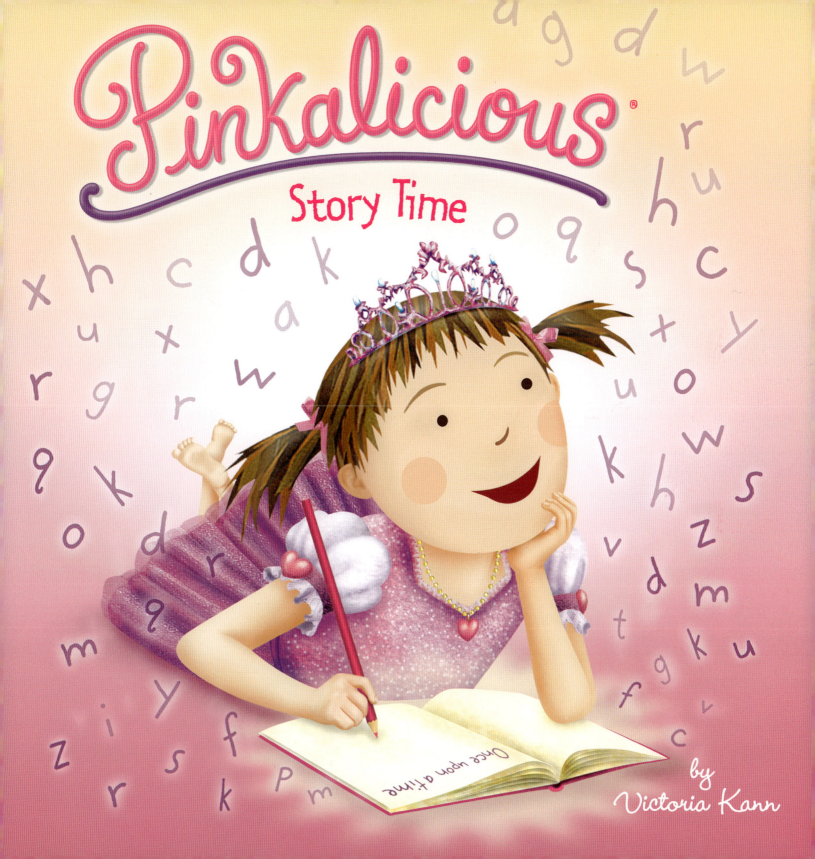

To Tamar

—V.K.

Story Time

by Victoria Kann

We were at a book fair,

waiting in line.

I was going to meet my hero,

Princess Plum!

I have all of her books.

Meet the
Author of
the
Princess
Plum
books.

Princess Plum is kind.

She is smart.

She grants magic wishes
and wears a sparkly purple tiara.

I love her stories.

"I hope she signs my book,"

I told Mommy.

I couldn't believe I was going to meet

a real princess at last.

But when we got

to the front of the line,

I was very surprised.

Instead of a princess, I saw a man!

"Is Princess Plum a man?" I said.

"I'm Syd Silver." The man laughed.

"I'm the author of Princess Plum.

That means I write books about her."

"But how can you write about
being a magic princess
if you aren't one?" I asked.
"When you're an author,
you can tell all sorts of stories,"
said Mr. Silver.

"Princess Plum is a character I made up.

Stories can be about anyone

or anything you want.

Just use your imagination!"

That afternoon,

I couldn't stop thinking

about what Mr. Silver had said.

I decided to give it a try.

I imagined I could fly

and wrote about soaring

around Pinkville.

In my story,

I made the clouds into cotton candy.

After that,

I wrote about a tea party

with dancing spoons and cups.

I wrote about a garden growing under my bed.

I wrote about a family of pirates that lives inside the washing machine.

I couldn't stop writing!

At dinnertime,

I wrote about a broccoli jungle

and sweet-potato mountains.

Broccoli jungle
Sweet-potato mountains

At bedtime,

I wrote about

a pair of bunny slippers

hopping all over the house.

Homework due
tomorrow.

At school on Monday,

I came up with more ideas.

I wrote them all down.

I was too busy to listen

to my teacher, Ms. Penny.

I was writing about a pink panda
when Ms. Penny tapped my shoulder.
"Pinkalicious," she said,
"what are you doing?"

I gulped.

I told Ms. Penny everything,

about meeting the author Syd Silver

and writing stories all day long.

"I'm sorry for not paying attention,"

I said.

"Well," said Ms. Penny,

"paying attention is very important.

But so is being creative.

I think I have an idea."

"Listen everybody," said Ms. Penny.
"This week,
you are all going to be authors!
We will have special writing time
so you can work on your stories.
And on Friday, we'll have
our own class book festival."

At recess, we talked about our ideas.

"I'm writing about a

penguin named Percy," said Molly.

"I'm writing about a family of giants

who live in the rain forest,"

said Rose.

Alison's book was the biggest surprise.

It didn't have any words!

She was making a comic-book story

with only pictures.

We worked hard all week.

I finished the story about flying

through the cotton-candy clouds.

I drew the cover and added
an "about the author" page.
"Pinkalicious is from Pinkville,"
I wrote.
"She loves writing, baking cupcakes,
and anything pink!"

On Friday,

we read our stories out loud.

We signed our books.

It was so much fun!

Before I went home,

I told Ms. Penny

I had one last thing to write.

Dear Mr. Silver,

You may not be a princess who grants wishes, but your books are full of magic. Thank you for helping me see that I am a writer too!

Pinkalicious

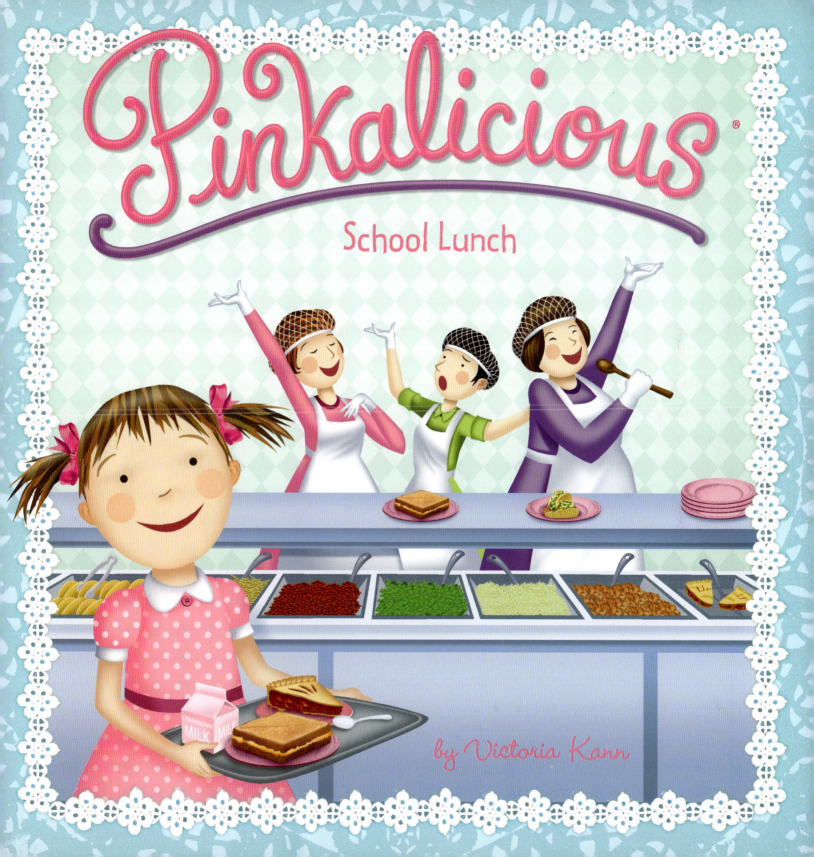

Pinkalicious

School Lunch

by Victoria Kann

If there's one thing I love for lunch,
it's a peanut butter and jelly sandwich.
Mommy packs it for me almost every day.

On Monday, I decided to try something totally different. I wanted to buy my lunch at the school cafeteria. It would be pinkerrific! They were serving spaghetti and meatballs with raspberry Jell-O for dessert. (Spaghetti looks pink if you use your imagination.)

At last, the bell rang.

"Lunchtime!" I yelled.

I leaped out of my seat and out the door, skipping down the hall at full speed. I was going so fast I didn't see the book on the floor. I tripped and fell and hurt my knee.

Ms. Penny came to help me. "Why the rush, Pinkalicious?" she asked.
I told her about the spaghetti and meatballs and pink Jell-O for dessert.
"Sounds yummy," she said. "But remember, slow and steady wins the race."
I wasn't sure what she meant, but I was too hungry to ask.

143

Ms. Penny walked down to the cafeteria with me. I got in line and waved good-bye. Soon enough, my special spaghetti would be all mine! All I had to do now was wait.

So I waited.

And waited.

And waited.

The line was so long it snaked around the cafeteria. We moved slowly, inch by inch. My tummy started grumbling. My knee throbbed. The room was noisier than I remembered. This was taking forever!

At long last, it was my turn to order. I cleared my throat and said,
"Spaghetti and meatballs with raspberry Jell-O, please!"

Ethel the lunch lady didn't hear me.

"Excuse me?" she said.

"Spaghetti and meatballs and Jell-O," I tried again.

It was no use. The room was too loud. Ethel shrugged and handed me a plate with green beans and a sloppy joe. No matter how hard I squinted, it did not look pink—or tasty.

I cleared my throat to try one last time, but just then, the bell rang. It was time to go back to class!

I couldn't believe what just happened. This was supposed to be my big day, my cafeteria feast! Now instead of spaghetti and meatballs and raspberry Jell-O, I had nothing but an empty stomach.

In math class, I had trouble paying attention. I was so hungry!
Triangles looked like pizza slices. Circles looked like pies.
When Ms. Penny showed us that a square cut diagonally makes two triangles,
I thought she was cutting a sandwich in half.
My tummy grumbled.

That night, I told Mommy and Daddy about how everything had gone wrong: how I had tripped and fallen, how I had hurt my knee, how it had taken forever to get through the line, and when I finally got there, the lunch lady couldn't hear my order.

"I'm sorry, honey," said Daddy.

"Would you like me to make you a peanut butter and jelly sandwich for tomorrow?" asked Mommy.

I didn't know what to do. Today did not turn out very well, but tomorrow they were serving grilled-cheese sandwiches. I like grilled cheese!

"I'll try again tomorrow, except this time, I'll be prepared," I said.

I finished my dinner and went up to my room. If I was going to actually eat the school lunch, I needed to have a plan.

The next day at school, when the lunch bell rang, I pulled out the plan I had made the night before.

"'Step one,'" I read out loud, "'watch your pace! Slow and steady wins the race.'" I made sure not to rush to the cafeteria, and this time, I made it without falling or bruising my knees. Ms. Penny was right—this was much better!

HAPPY DAY!!!

153

At the cafeteria, I got in line and looked around. There were still lots of kids ahead of me! I started getting frustrated, but then I remembered my plan. I was prepared.

"'Step two,'" I read. "'If the line is long, just sing a song.'" I began singing to pass the time.

I made it through *Pinkle, Pinkle, Little Star* and *Mary Had a Pink Ole Lamb*, and was just about finished with *Old PinkDonald* before I realized I was almost at the front of the line.

"Are you singing something?" asked Ethel the lunch lady. I started to answer her, but the cafeteria was so loud she couldn't hear me.

That's when I knew it was time for step three of my plan.

"Is the room very noisy from the lunch-eating crowd? Then roll up this plan, and speak up real loud," it said.

I rolled my plan into a megaphone. I put it up to my mouth and asked for a grilled-cheese sandwich and a piece of pie.

"Huh?" said Ethel. Even with a megaphone, she still couldn't hear me!

157

Hmmm, I thought. *She could hear me when I was singing! I know. . . .*

"May I please have a grilled cheese and a piece of cherry pie?" I sang.

This time, Ethel heard me.

"Yes, you may!" Ethel sang back, handing me the cherry pie.

"Here's your grilled cheese," sang the other lunch lady, giving me another plate.

"And how about some strawberry milk?" sang the third lunch lady.

"Thank you!" I sang back.

"You are welcome!" sang the three lunch ladies in perfect harmony.

The cafeteria was completely quiet as everyone listened to them sing.
When they finished, everyone clapped and yelled, "Hooray!"
The whole room filled up with our cheers. The lunch lady trio took a bow.
I sat down and finally got to eat my cafeteria feast!

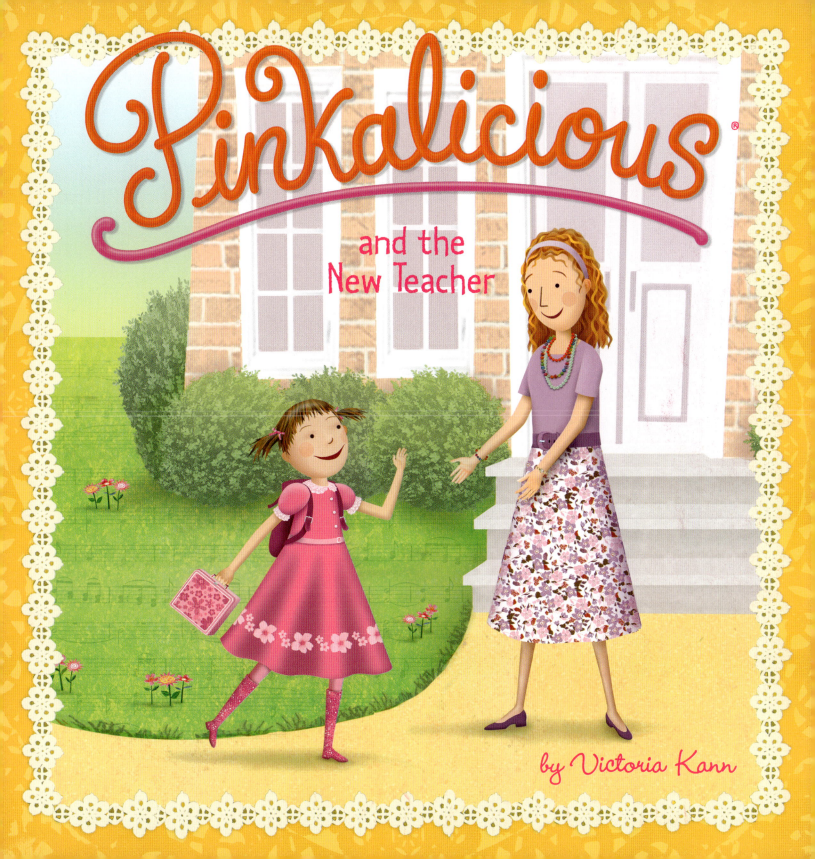

Pinkalicious

and the New Teacher

by Victoria Kann

With love and gratitude to our teachers
—V.K.

Pinkalicious

and the New Teacher

by Victoria Kann

It was the first day of school, and I couldn't wait to show my friends my new sparkly boots and pinkatastic lunch box. I was so excited about my new pink accessories, I forgot something else would be brand new. . . .

Ms. Penny

"Welcome! My name is Ms. Penny," said my new teacher. "Please find your name on the table and take a seat."

Welcome back, students!

Rose

Alison

Penny ⭐

Welcome back,
students!

Rose

Alison

170

I looked for my seat. It was all the way across the room from my best friend, Alison.

"Last year, we got to choose where to sit," I told Ms. Penny.

Ms. Penny smiled and said, "New seats, new people to meet."

My chair was in the corner. I hate the corner.

MONTHS OF THE YEAR

January	July
February	August
March	September
April	October
May	November
June	December

It had started to rain, so we had indoor recess. Alison and I drew a pinknificent palace on the chalkboard.

"Splendid, Princess Alison!" I said. "However, it's not a castle without a royal unicorn in a royal garden."

"True, your Royal Pinkness," said Alison. "Shall we plant pink roses or pink peonies?"
"Both!" I told her.

"Look how happy your unicorn looks in the sunny garden you drew!" Ms. Penny exclaimed.

Ms. Penny might be okay after all.

Count by 2: 2 4 6 8

Count by 5: 5 10 15 20

Count by 1 10 20 30

After lunch, we went back to the classroom. I couldn't believe my eyes. The pink palace and unicorn were gone! Our masterpieces had been erased.

Ms. Penny isn't okay at all—I wanted my old teacher back!

"It's story time!" Ms. Penny announced later that afternoon. I looked around.

"Ms. Penny, it can't be story time!" I said. "Last year, we always had story time on the comfy, shaggy reading rug."

"I'm sorry, Pinkalicious, but I don't have a shaggy reading rug. I do have beanbag chairs, though. They're not shaggy, but they are comfy."

"It's not the same."

"Try it. I have a story I think you're going to like."

I wiggled in the crinkly beanbag chair as Ms. Penny read about a girl named Pinkalina who was as big as a pinky finger.

After story time, Ms. Penny told us to write about our summer adventures. My old teacher used to draw smiley faces on our papers. Ms. Penny gave me a star sticker. I liked the star, but I missed getting a smiley face.

This summer I went to the seashore with my family.

name: Pinkalicious

I crossed my arms, slumped in my chair, and scowled at the table.

January   July
February   August
March   September
April   October
May   November
June   December

"Pinkalicious, is everything okay?" Ms. Penny asked.

"I miss sitting next to Alison, and I miss the reading rug and getting smiley faces on my class work."

"The day hasn't been all bad. I saw you laugh during *Pinkalina*. I'm sorry I erased your pictures, but I needed the board for class."

I sighed. "I just miss last year."

"Is there something that your old teacher used to do that we might be able to do this year?"

I thought. Then I got an idea—a PINKERRIFIC idea.

"Pinkalicious told me that your previous teacher used to decorate the classroom," Ms. Penny said. "Any suggestions on how we should beautify the room this year?"

"Let's draw animals and make the room look like a jungle," Rose said.

"What if we draw dinosaurs?" Alex suggested.

I raised my hand. "I know!" I said. "Let's draw ourselves!"
The entire class loved my idea.

Ms. Penny taped paper to the wall and handed out markers. We took turns outlining each other, then decorated the life-size portraits of ourselves.

I drew myself as the Princess of Pink. I was glad my masterpiece couldn't be erased. When we were done, the room looked exciting and colorful.

Ms. Penny wasn't so bad. I thought I was going to like my new teacher. In fact, she was pretty pinkamazing.

We all looked at Ms. Penny's portrait. . . .

She was the Queen of Pink!

MONTHS OF THE YEAR

January	July
February	August
March	September
April	October
May	November
June	December

MONTHS OF THE YEAR

January	July
February	August
March	September
April	October
May	November
June	December

The author gratefully acknowledges the artistic and editorial contributions of Daniel Griffo, Susan Hill, Dynamo, Loryn Brantz, Kirsten Berger, Natalie Engel, Kamilla Benko, and Robert Masheris.

Have you read all of these *Pinkalicious*® books yet?

- ☐ Pinkalicious
- ☐ Purplicious
- ☐ Goldilicious
- ☐ Silverlicious
- ☐ Emeraldalicious
- ☐ Aqualicious
- ☐ Peterrific
- ☐ Pinkalicious: Love, Pinkalicious
- ☐ Pinkalicious and the Pink Drink
- ☐ Pinkalicious: School Rules!
- ☐ Pinkalicious: Tickled Pink
- ☐ Pinkalicious: Pink around the Rink
- ☐ Pinkalicious: The Perfectly Pink Collection
- ☐ Pinkalicious: Pinkadoodles
- ☐ Pinkalicious: Pinkie Promise
- ☐ Pinkalicious and the Pink Pumpkin

- ☐ Pinkalicious: The Pinkerrific Playdate
- ☐ Pinkalicious: The Princess of Pink Treasury
- ☐ Pinkalicious: Pink of Hearts
- ☐ Pinkalicious: The Pinkatastic Giant Sticker Book
- ☐ Pinkalicious: The Princess of Pink Slumber Party
- ☐ Pinkalicious and the Pink Hat Parade
- ☐ Pinkalicious: Soccer Star
- ☐ Pinkalicious: Pink-a-rama
- ☐ Pinkalicious: Purpledoodles
- ☐ Pinkalicious: Pink, Pink, Hooray!
- ☐ Pinkalicious and the Pinkatastic Zoo Day
- ☐ Pinkalicious: Teeny Tiny Pinky Library
- ☐ Pinkalicious: Flower Girl
- ☐ Pinkalicious: Fairy House
- ☐ Pinkalicious: Pinkafy Your World
- ☐ Pinkalicious: Puptastic!
- ☐ Pinkalicious: Pink or Treat!
- ☐ Pinkalicious: Goldidoodles
- ☐ Pinkalicious: Merry Pinkmas!
- ☐ Pinkalicious and the Cupcake Calamity
- ☐ Pinkalicious Cupcake Cookbook
- ☐ Pinkalicious and the Perfect Present
- ☐ Pinkalicious: Eggstraordinary Easter
- ☐ Pinkalicious and the New Teacher
- ☐ Pinkalicious: The Royal Tea Party
- ☐ Pinkalicious: Crazy Hair Day
- ☐ Pinkalicious: Thanksgiving Helper
- ☐ Pinkalicious: Tutu-rrific

- ☐ Pinkalicious: Cherry Blossom
- ☐ Pinkalicious: Mother's Day Surprise
- ☐ Pinkalicious and the Pink Parakeet
- ☐ Pinkalicious Phonics Box Set
- ☐ Pinkalicious: School Lunch
- ☐ Pinkalicious and the Snow Globe
- ☐ Pinkalicious and the Sick Day
- ☐ Pinkalicious Take-Along Storybook Set
- ☐ Pinkalicious and the Little Butterfly
- ☐ Pinkalicious and Planet Pink
- ☐ Pinkalicious: Story Time
- ☐ Pinkalicious and Aqua, the Mini-Mermaid
- ☐ Pinkalicious: Fashion Fun
- ☐ Pinkalicious ABC
- ☐ Pinkalicious 123
- ☐ Pinkalicious: Apples, Apples, Apples!
- ☐ Pinkalicious and the Babysitter
- ☐ Pinkalicious at the Fair
- ☐ Pinkalicious: 5-Minute Pinkalicious Stories
- ☐ Pinkalicious and the Pirates
- ☐ Pinkalicious and the Amazing Sled Run
- ☐ Pinkalicious and the Flower Fairy
- ☐ Pinkalicious: Fishtastic!
- ☐ Pinkalicious: Dragon to the Rescue
- ☐ Pinkalicious: Pinkamazing Storybook Favorites
- ☐ Pinkalicious and the Merminnies